# Eerie
## Elementary

# The Hall Monitors Are FIRED!

By Jack Chabert
Illustrated by Matt Loveridge,
based on the art of Sam Ricks

BRANCHES

SCHOLASTIC INC.

# READ ALL THE
## Eerie Elementary
# ADVENTURES!

# TABLE OF CONTENTS

# For Lila — JC

Text copyright © 2018 by Max Brallier
Illustrations by Matt Loveridge copyright © 2018 by Scholastic Inc.

Library of Congress Cataloging-in-Publication Data

Names: Chabert, Jack, author. | Loveridge, Matt, illustrator. | Chabert,
Jack. Eerie Elementary ; 8.
Title: The hall monitors are fired! / by Jack Chabert ; illustrated by Matt
Loveridge.
Description: New York : Branches/Scholastic Inc., 2018. | Series: Eerie
Elementary ; 8 | Summary: Sam Graves and his friends Lucy and Antonio have
used their positions as hall monitors to thwart Orson Eerie's attacks on
the students of Eerie Elementary—but now Orson is determined to get them
fired before his next attack, planned for the annual Kickball Showdown.
Identifiers: LCCN 2017021916| ISBN 9781338181883 (pbk. : alk. paper) |
ISBN 9781338181913 (hardcover : alk. paper)
Subjects: LCSH: Haunted schools—Juvenile fiction. | Elementary
schools—Juvenile fiction. | Kickball—Juvenile fiction. | Best
friends—Juvenile fiction. | Horror tales. | CYAC: Haunted
places—Fiction. | Schools—Fiction. | Kickball—Fiction. | Best
friends—Fiction. | Friendship. | Horror stories.
Classification: LCC PZ7.C3313 Hal 2018 | DDC 813.6 [Fic] —dc23 LC record available at
https://lccn.loc.gov/2017021916

10 9 8 7 6 5 4 3 2 1        18 19 20 21 22

Printed in China    38
First edition, May 2018
Illustrated by Matt Loveridge
Edited by Katie Carella
Book design by Maria Mercado

# A MERRY MORNING

"I can't wait for tomorrow!" Sam Graves said to himself as he strolled through the Eerie Elementary school gate.

Sam had a huge smile on his face. The sun was warm and the grass was green. Best of all, tomorrow was Sam's favorite day of the year: Kickball Showdown!

Sam spotted his best friends, Antonio and Lucy. They were on the front steps of the school, helping students line up. Today they had morning hall monitor duty.

Sam was Eerie Elementary's head hall monitor, and Antonio and Lucy were assistant hall monitors. They did normal things, like make sure their classmates behaved in the hallways and help students line up before the morning bell. But they also did *top-secret* things . . .

**RING!!!**

*The bell!* Sam thought. *I'd better hurry!*

Sam threw on his hall monitor sash as he sped across the playground.

Students funneled into the school. Sam was about to call out to Antonio and Lucy, but —

**SMACK!**

"Oof!" Sam exclaimed. He crashed to the ground! Thankfully, a bed of wood chips cushioned his fall. Sam looked to see what had made him trip. His shoelace was hooked on the merry-go-round.

*How did my shoelace get caught there?* Sam wondered. He reached to unhook his shoelace. But then —

**YANK!**

"Whoa!" Sam shouted. He was suddenly *dragged* across the ground. The rusty merry-go-round was turning. All by itself! With every squeak, it jerked Sam roughly across the dry wood chips.

Sam's heart pounded. He hadn't tripped — the merry-go-round had *grabbed* his shoelace. This was the work of Orson Eerie.

Sam was one of the few people who knew the truth about Eerie Elementary: The school was alive!

Nearly 100 years ago, a mad scientist named Orson Eerie found a way to live forever — he *became* the school. Orson Eerie was the school, and the school was Orson Eerie! Eerie Elementary was a living, breathing thing that *fed* on students. And hall monitor Sam Graves was the protector of its students and teachers.

ORSON EERIE 1871-?

Glancing up, Sam saw his third-grade teacher, Ms. Grinker, in the school doorway.

*Maybe I can get her attention!* Sam thought. He tried to call her name, but he was spinning too fast to get the words out. He scraped and tore at the wood chips, but it was useless. The merry-go-round wasn't slowing down.

Ms. Grinker stepped inside. The door shut.

*Now I'm alone out here!* Sam thought. *Alone with a monstrous merry-go-round!*

**SQUEAK! SCREECH! SQUEAL!**

The rickety, rusty merry-go-round spun like a top. Sam clawed at the wood chips, but the speed caused him to be lifted off the ground. His arms waved about wildly. He felt the wind in his hair as he spun faster and faster.

"Oh no!" Sam gasped. At any moment, the merry-go-round would release him — and he'd go flying!

# RUNNING LATE

$S$am's heart slammed in his chest. The merry-go-round spun and spun!

The speed plus the force made Sam's sneaker squeeze his foot tighter and tighter!

He shouted, "SOMEONE HELP!"

But the playground was empty.

Sam's mind raced. *I'm going to be thrown from this thing! I can't stop it!*

But then —

**CLANK-CA-CLANK!**

The rusty merry-go-round shuddered and slowed! Sam crashed into the wood chips. His shoelace was released. He staggered to his feet. He had never been dizzier.

*The school could have hurled me,* Sam thought. *But it didn't. The school has never let me go without a fight before . . .*

Sam was confused — but he was also late! He raced toward the school. He bounded up the steps and hurried inside.

"Sam Graves!" Ms. Grinker barked as he ran into the classroom. "You're *late*. Our head hall monitor should *never* be tardy."

Sam felt his face grow red. Everyone was staring. A few students chuckled.

"I'm sorry," Sam said quickly. He made his way to his desk, next to Antonio and Lucy.

"Hey, buddy. You're never late," Antonio whispered.

Lucy added, "What happened?"

Sam was about to explain, but Ms. Grinker shot him a look.

"Students: a reminder!" said Ms. Grinker. "Tomorrow is the annual Kickball Showdown. As always, the game will have five innings. Two teams will take turns kicking and fielding. The team that scores the most runs wins."

The class began buzzing. Everyone loved Kickball Showdown.

Ms. Grinker continued, "Our class will compete against Ms. Armstrong's third-grade class. The entire school will watch from the bleachers."

"I am *pumped*," Antonio whispered to Sam. "I have been practicing my diving face-first slide. I'm going to steal a base!"

"I'll believe it when I see it," Lucy said, smiling. "You might just trip and splat!"

"No way!" Antonio said. "It will be the perfect slide — in front of the whole school!"

Sam's heart pounded. *The whole school,* he thought. *Kickball Showdown means the whole school will be in one place!*

That morning, for the first time ever, Eerie Elementary had simply let Sam go. And tomorrow, the whole school would be gathered in one place for the big game. Sam was certain *both* things were part of *one big* Orson Eerie evil plan.

Sam gulped. He no longer felt *excited* for Kickball Showdown. Now, he felt *afraid* . . .

# FROM BAD TO WORSE

Sam's day got worse and worse. In fact, it was an awful day for all three of Eerie Elementary's hall monitors!

First, Lucy got in trouble. She was holding the door when it *jumped* from her hand — and slammed in Ms. Grinker's face! It looked like Lucy had slammed the door on purpose. Ms. Grinker gave her a warning.

Antonio got in trouble next. It was just before recess and everyone was at their lockers. Antonio set his backpack down, but it *leapt* into the middle of the hallway — right beneath Ms. Grinker's feet! She scolded him, too.

"It feels like the school is *trying* to get us in trouble," Antonio said to his friends as they walked outside.

During recess, things got worse . . .

The hall monitors were by the jungle gym when Mr. Nekobi walked over. Mr. Nekobi was the old man who took care of Eerie Elementary. It was Mr. Nekobi who had chosen Sam to be the school's hall monitor. He had shown Sam the horrible truth about the monstrous school.

Mr. Nekobi said, "I have to trim some trees in front of the school. Would you three mind getting the field ready for Kickball Showdown?"

"Sure! Lucy and I can set up the bleachers," Antonio said.

"I'll clean off the bases and inflate the kickballs," Sam said.

He grabbed a broom and followed his friends to the field.

Sam was sweeping home plate when he felt a twisting and tangling inside his gut. As hall monitor, Sam could sense things that other students couldn't. He could *feel* when something was wrong. Right now, Sam had that feeling.

He looked up. The metal backstop loomed over him.

**CREEE-EEEE-EEAK!**

Wind whipped across the field and the backstop shook. Sunlight danced and shined on the metal fence.

Sam couldn't pull his eyes away from it. He felt like he was falling into a trance . . .

Sam saw *a face.* It was the face of his ultimate enemy: Orson Eerie. And the face was staring at Sam!

**RING!**

The sound snapped Sam out of his trance.

"That's the bell, Sam!" Lucy yelled. "We need to head inside!"

"But I still need to inflate the kickballs!" Sam called back.

"We'll help!" Antonio shouted. He and Lucy hurried over.

Sam grabbed an air pump and inflated the kickballs. Lucy and Antonio helped. They were finishing when —

RING!

"The second bell!" Sam exclaimed. "Now we're *really* late!"

Sam placed the pump near the bleachers. Then he and his friends raced inside. But they soon skidded to a stop.

Ms. Grinker was waiting for them in the classroom doorway. Their classmates were already seated.

"I'm fed up with you three!" Ms. Grinker barked. "Sam, you've been late *twice* today. Lucy, Antonio — your behavior has been unacceptable!"

"But —" Sam began.

She interrupted him. "As punishment, you will all stay after school today. You will scrape the gum from beneath every classroom desk."

Sam's classmates said, "OOOOOH."

Ms. Grinker glared at Sam, Antonio, and Lucy. "You'd better shape up — *or you won't be hall monitors much longer!*"

# SPOOKY SCRUBBING

**4**

School was over — and the messy job of scraping gum had begun.

Ms. Grinker was at her desk grading papers. She looked up every few moments, keeping an eye on the three students.

Sam was on his back, staring up at a desk. Dozens of hard, dried bubble gum blobs dotted the desk's bottom.

"Gross," he muttered.

Antonio and Lucy were underneath desks, too.

"Who chewed all this gum?!" Antonio whispered.

"Not me," Lucy replied.

They each used a wooden ruler to chip away at the bright neon-colored gum. Flaky bits of dried gum sprinkled down onto their faces.

Ms. Grinker stood. "I am heading to the teachers' lounge. When I return, every desk had better be gum-free!"

Ms. Grinker shut the door. Instantly, Sam's gut felt tight. It was the same feeling he'd had earlier . . .

CLATTER!
CLATTER!
CLATTER!

"Sam! Your desk!" Lucy said.

The desk above Sam was *shaking*. The metal feet rattled. It was practically jumping! And then —

# CLANK! ZOOM!

The desk leapt into the air!

Sam rolled out of the way just before —

SLAM!

The desk crashed to the floor.

Lucy and Antonio scrambled out from beneath their desks.

"Stay calm!" Antonio said.

"Easy for you to say," Sam replied. "It was MY desk that did a backflip!"

"Wait . . . what's that?" asked Lucy.

The friends inched toward the overturned desk. A purple blob of gum was bubbling on the bottom of the desk. It seemed to be growing bigger and bigger.

Then — **WHOOSH!**

A lump of wet gum *whipped* past Sam's face! He whirled around. Chunks of gum were flying across the room! It was like invisible hands were throwing them!

Hundreds of globs of gum started joining together! A massive, monstrous ball of gum was forming.

"What's happening?!" Lucy asked.

"Whatever it is, I don't want to be here for it!" Antonio said.

"Follow me!" Sam sped toward the door. But suddenly, a gummy tentacle *cracked* like a whip.

**SLAP!**

It snapped against Sam's wrist and encircled his arm! The sticky tentacle hurled Sam into a bookshelf.

"Sam!" Lucy cried out.

More neon-colored tentacles leapt from the gigantic ball and snaked toward Sam! They yanked him off his feet.

"The gum has got me!" Sam cried.

Sam kicked and fought, but he just became more stuck! Orange and pink gum surrounded him. He was sinking into the great gummy beast!

# CHEWED OUT!

## 5

The monstrous wad of bubble gum was about to swallow Sam whole! He couldn't wrestle free from the sticky mess.

Lucy's eyes bulged. "Sam's being gobbled up by a bubble gum monster!"

Wet strands of bubble gum slithered across Sam's face. The stink of sticky sweetness filled his nostrils.

Soon, only bits of Sam were visible. One sneaker jutted out from the huge, colorful ball. Two hands poked through the mess.

"*We're* supposed to chew gum!" Antonio said. "Gum isn't supposed to chew *us*!"

"We have to pull him out!" Lucy cried.

They dashed toward their friend. Antonio grabbed Sam's hand. Lucy took Sam's foot. They pulled and tugged and —

Sam tumbled out of the bubble gum monster. The three friends crashed into Ms. Grinker's desk.

**GLOOOG-OOOOO-WHOO!**

A wet, monstrous *howl* filled the room.

"It's not over yet!" Sam yelled.

Lucy's eyes went wide. "It looks like the monster is turning into one giant bubble gum BUBBLE!"

The swelling pink globe was filling the classroom! Desks tumbled over. A bookshelf crashed to the floor.

Sam could see the doorway through the bubble, but escape was impossible!

"Get behind Ms. Grinker's desk!" Sam called out.

The friends scrambled over the desk. But the moment their feet hit the ground, the bubble pushed the desk. It pinned them against the board!

Ms. Grinker's red pen started rolling away. Antonio and Lucy quickly reached for it — and banged heads.

"Are you thinking what I'm thinking?" Lucy asked.

"Yep!" Antonio said. "Pop that bubble!"

Lucy scooped up the pen and held it like a tiny sword. The bubble grew bigger and came closer.

Lucy thrust the pen into the bubble. **POP!**

It burst! It was the biggest blast of bubble gum in the history of bubble gum blasts! Sticky, gooey mess splattered everywhere.

"Yuck!" Lucy exclaimed, as she pulled gum from her hair.

**SLAM!**

The door flew open. Ms. Grinker's eyes bulged as she stared at the strange mess. Gum dripped from the walls. Strings of pink and orange goo hung from the ceiling.

Ms. Grinker was furious. Sam wouldn't have been surprised if steam started coming out of her ears!

"That's it!" Ms. Grinker roared. "You are DONE being hall monitors!"

# HANDING IT OVER

"Bubble gum is everywhere!" Ms. Grinker exclaimed in Principal Winik's office. "I don't know *how* three third graders created such a HUGE, sticky mess!"

Sam, Lucy, and Antonio stood before their principal. Ms. Grinker was arguing that they should be *fired* from their hall monitor jobs. Principal Winik's mouth was a tight, stern line. Mr. Nekobi was there, too. He had been listening silently, but now he stepped forward.

"Principal Winik," Mr. Nekobi began. "Sam is a very responsible hall monitor. And Lucy and Antonio are the best assistant hall monitors this school has ever had."

Ms. Grinker scowled. "Lucy closed a door in my face!"

"It wasn't my —" Lucy started.

Ms. Grinker interrupted. "And Antonio tripped me!"

"I didn't —" Antonio began to say.

Ms. Grinker slammed her hands down on Principal Winik's desk. "Being a hall monitor is a very special privilege. Students who get detention, who are tardy, and who cause bubble gum explosions *cannot* be hall monitors!"

Principal Winik stood up. "I agree. You three are FIRED! Sam, please turn in your sash."

Sam swallowed. He couldn't believe this was happening.

Sam's hand trembled as he pulled the bright orange sash from his backpack. Mr. Nekobi had given him the sash on his first day as hall monitor. It was a symbol of the hall monitors' power.

The moment he handed it to Principal Winik, Sam felt weak. He felt like the wind had been knocked out of him.

Sam remembered what Mr. Nekobi had told him, months earlier: "As hall monitor, you have the ability to *sense* the school — to see and feel and hear what others cannot."

Principal Winik stuffed the sash into a desk drawer. "One last thing," he said. "Sam, Lucy, Antonio: You will *not* be participating in tomorrow's Kickball Showdown. Instead, you three will scrub your classroom until it sparkles."

Sam and his friends slunk down the hall. Mr. Nekobi followed them outside. Spring was just around the corner and the air was warm.

"The school hasn't been left unprotected like this in years . . ." Mr. Nekobi said.

"Unprotected? I don't understand," Lucy said. "We're still *here*. We can still fight."

Mr. Nekobi's voice was heavy and sad. "Yes. But you are no longer hall monitors. I'm afraid you simply won't be strong enough to battle Eerie Elementary."

Sam and his friends dragged their feet as they walked home.

"I can't believe we lost our jobs," Lucy said. "How did we let this happen?"

"We didn't *let* anything happen," Sam said. "Orson Eerie messed with us all day and made us look like terrible hall monitors!"

Antonio scowled. "It's like the school was *trying* to get us fired!"

"Well, it worked!" Lucy said. "We were fired just in time for —"

"Kickball Showdown!" they exclaimed at once.

"This *was* all part of Orson's plan!" Sam said. He looked back at the old, towering school. "We know what Orson wants. The same thing he always wants. To eat . . ."

Sam's words hung in the air. What he said was true — and terrifying. In fact, it was *so terrifying* that Sam and his friends walked the rest of the way home in frightened silence.

# UP, UP, AND AWAY

Principal Winik's voice boomed through the open classroom window: **"Teams, please take the field!"**

It was the next morning and Kickball Showdown was beginning. Sam, Lucy, and Antonio were stuck inside, scrubbing gum.

"I feel like Cinderella," Antonio said, as he scraped gum from a window.

"Yeah, but instead of missing some fancy ball, we are missing Kickball Showdown," Lucy added.

"No talking!" Ms. Grinker barked. She was at her desk (which was *covered* in gum).

She stood and marched across the room. "I'm going to straighten up the supply closet. But I will be watching this door! If anyone leaves, you're in *big trouble*!"

The door shut.

**WOOOT!** A whistle pierced the air.

Principal Winik's whistle announced the start of the first inning.

Sam, Lucy, and Antonio ran to the window. Teachers and students were seated in the bleachers.

"Everyone's out there!" Antonio said.

"And there are no hall monitors to stop Orson from attacking!" Lucy said.

"Guys, we need to find a way to protect everyone," Sam said.

Antonio peeked out the door window. He saw Ms. Grinker at the supply closet. "How can we sneak out while she's right there?"

Just then — **SPLAT!**

A glob of blue bubble gum dropped onto Sam's shoulder. He glanced up. A string of gum dangled from an air vent in the ceiling.

Sam smiled. "If we don't walk out that door, Ms. Grinker won't know we're gone!"

A moment later, he was standing on a desk. Antonio and Lucy were hoisting him up, into the vent . . .

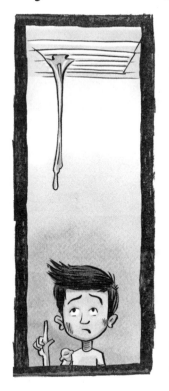

# TERRIFYING TEETH!

**8**

"**Y**esterday we were in a sticky situation," Antonio said. "Now we're in a tight spot!"

Sam, Lucy, and Antonio were crawling through the air vent. They had to wiggle and wriggle to move forward.

"Uh-oh," Sam said. "The vent splits up ahead. Which way will take us closest to the front of the school? Right or left?"

"Let me check!" Lucy called. "I brought the blueprints of the school."

Lucy peered through a crack in the vent. She saw they were above the art room. She squinted to read the blueprints, using them like a map.

"Principal Winik's office is near the front doors — so let's go there," she said, as she ran her finger over the blueprint. "Take a right here, then a left at the gym, and another left at the lunchroom."

Sam crawled to the right.

They heard Principal Winik's voice from outside: **"The second inning starts now!"**

"Oh no!" Antonio said. "It's already the second inning! There are only three innings left! Orson's going to attack soon!"

"We need to hurry!" Lucy said.

Sam scrambled forward. The smells of the lunchroom drifted into the vent. That meant they were close! Sam wormed his way around the corner. He felt a cool breeze rushing up from an opening.

He saw Principal Winik's desk far below. "We're here!" Sam said.

He tried to gently climb down, but instead —
**CRUNCH!**

His hand plunged through the vent! He crash-landed on Principal Winik's desk.

"Oof," Sam groaned. He blinked and saw Antonio and Lucy peering down at him.

"Nice landing!" Lucy joked.

Sam stood. He helped Lucy and Antonio down from the vent.

Suddenly, Sam felt like there was something he *had* to do . . . He yanked open Principal Winik's desk drawer. "I'm taking *this* back!" he said, and he grabbed the sash.

Relief flooded through him.

Lucy and Antonio smiled at their friend.

"Now let's get to the kickball field and stop Orson Eerie!" Lucy said.

She ran out into the hallway. Antonio followed. But as Sam stepped through the office door —

The wood cracked! The door was like a chomping mouth with splintery fangs!

"Watch out!" Antonio yelled.

**SNAP!** The door's terrifying teeth bit the sash! Sam held one end and the monstrous mouth had the other!

# IN A JAM

The chomping door held the sash in its splintery teeth.

"I can't get it free!" Sam cried.

Lucy and Antonio grabbed onto Sam. They pulled hard, but the door had slammed shut like a mousetrap. It wouldn't let go!

"Orson Eerie *really* doesn't want you to have your sash back!" Lucy cried.

Sam glanced at his friends. They knew that without the sash, they wouldn't be strong enough to defeat the school.

Sam dug his fingers into the fabric.

"Everyone, PULL!" he shouted.

They tugged with all their might!

A moment later, Sam, Lucy, and Antonio tumbled to the floor. The sash was tattered, but it was still in one piece.

Sam leapt to his feet. He looked around: at the walls, at the ceiling, down the long hall. He thrust the sash in the air. "Listen up, Orson Eerie!" he shouted. "You'll *never* get rid of us!"

"Come on!" Lucy yelled, tugging on Sam's sleeve. "Orson could strike the game at any moment!"

Principal Winik's voice rang out: **"The third inning starts now!"**

Sam and his friends hurried around the corner. They ran toward the double doors at the end of the hall.

But then Sam felt it.

Orson Eerie wasn't giving up without a fight . . .

The floor rippled. The walls trembled.

"Am I crazy?" Antonio asked. "Or is the hall getting *smaller*?"

Sam realized it was true. The hallway was narrowing. The walls were closing in around them!

"Orson's trying to use *the hall* to defeat the *hall monitors*?!" Lucy said.

"Run!" Antonio cried.

The floors swayed and shifted as the friends barreled down the hall.

KRAKA-BURST!

Sam glanced upward. The shrinking hall had knocked all the water sprinklers in the ceiling loose. Ice-cold water gushed down! The floor was soaking wet.

The friends leaned forward and ran harder. But the doors seemed to be getting farther and farther away. The hallway was lengthening!

**AIEEEE!**

The hallway shrieked as the walls closed around them.

Sam's heart raced. *We're going to be crushed!*

# LET IT SLIDE

## 10

Just minutes earlier, the hallway had been normal and wide. But now it was much skinnier — and shrinking. Sam felt a locker pressing against his shoulder.

"If we're crushed by this hallway, I'll never get to show off my cool Kickball Showdown sliding skills!" Antonio cried as they ran.

**SPLOOSH! SPLOOSH!**

Sam noticed his sneakers splish-splashing in the rising water. "Antonio, you just gave me an idea!" Sam said with a smile. "We'll *slide* out of here!"

"The sprinklers *did* sort of turn the hallway into a water slide!" Lucy exclaimed.

Sam glanced back. The walls were squeezing shut behind them.

"I'll lead the way!" Antonio said. He dove forward and splashed down onto the floor. Sam and Lucy did the same —

**VA-ZOOM!**

The three friends zipped down the hall!

Water rushed up, splashing Sam's face. He held his breath so he wouldn't get water up his nose.

Sam felt Lucy and Antonio squished against him as they slid down the hall.

"This hallway is crushing us!" Sam cried.

"And it keeps getting smaller!" Lucy yelled.

The walls were closing in, and Sam could *hear* Orson Eerie. He could *hear* the school.

It was the school's heart! It beat harder and harder as the friends zoomed toward the double doors at the end of the hall.

Ba BUMP!
Ba BUMP!
Ba BUMP!

Orson Eerie's cry was deafening as they sped down the hall. The walls were so tight that it felt like Orson was shrieking in their ears.

"We're almost there!" Antonio cried.

Sam lifted his head. Squinting through the spray of water, he saw the double doors. He and his friends were going to crash into them!

HOWLLLL!!!

They slid toward the doors at top speed.

"Brace for impact!" Sam shouted, and he threw his hands over his head.

POP!

# STORMING MAD

## 11

The double doors burst open! Sam, Lucy, and Antonio tumbled out onto the stone steps.

Sam took a moment to catch his breath. Then he asked, "Is everyone okay?"

"Okay?!" Antonio asked. "I'm awesome! I *nailed* that slide!"

Sam grinned as he stood. He was soaking wet, but he didn't care. They were finally outside.

## "FOURTH INNING!"

"There is only *one* inning left!" Lucy said. "The game's almost over!"

Sam peered around the corner of the school. He saw the kickball field and the crowded bleachers.

"We need to get over there," Sam said.

"We also need to stay out of sight," Antonio added.

All of a sudden, there was a loud **WHOOMP**. One of their classmates had kicked a home run. The crowd cheered and watched the ball fly through the air.

"Now, run!" Sam said. "While no one's looking!"

The friends sped toward the field, then ducked down and ran beneath the bleachers. They peered through the metal planks. They could see the action on the field — but no one could see them.

Antonio gasped. "Look! I think Orson's doing stuff!"

Sam and Lucy saw it, too. There was a player standing on first base. But the base suddenly moved on its own! The player slipped.

Next, the pitcher's mound trembled.

Antonio started toward the field. But Sam stopped him. "Wait! What if Orson is doing small things to try to get us out on the field?"

"Like a trap?" Antonio asked.

"Right," Lucy said. "If we run out there, everyone will see us. Principal Winik will totally bust us. We'd never get our jobs back."

Antonio clenched his fists. "So we wait . . . The big attack must still be coming."

As Antonio said that, a gust of wind blew across the field. Grass swirled. The backstop rattled. The soft brown dirt of the base paths was lifted into the air.

At second base, a player's cap was plucked from her head.

"DUST STORM!" someone cried out.

Sam looked up.

He saw a dark cloud gathering over the field. But Sam knew the truth. This wasn't an ordinary dust storm. This was the work of Orson Eerie!

# PLAY BALL!

12

The strange dust storm grew bigger. More and more dirt whirled and spun in the air. A kickball was sucked into the storm. Teachers wiped at their eyes. Students spit out dirt.

"This is crazy!" Sam cried from beneath the bleachers.

"We need to do something!" Lucy shouted over the wind.

Just then, Mr. Nekobi bounded onto the field. "Principal Winik! You must call off the game!" he shouted.

"Yes!" Principal Winik yelled, as he shielded himself from the storm. "Teachers: Please lead your students inside!"

Dirt pounded the metal backstop like thundering rain. The swirling dirt made it difficult for the teachers to collect their students.

From his hiding place, Sam watched kids rush around. He squinted as Mr. Nekobi led the parade of teachers and students off the field and into the school.

"Phew," Lucy said. "It looks like everyone made it inside."

**WHAP! WHAP! WHAP!**

The wind beat across the field. The storm settled above the pitcher's mound.

"HELP!" a voice shouted over the wind.

Sam saw that one student was still on the field: a kindergartner named Ollie.

The dirt was whipping around and Ollie shielded his eyes. The boy couldn't see Sam and his friends.

"Oh no!" Sam said. "Ollie was left behind!"

Lucy rushed out from under the bleachers and sprinted onto the field. Antonio and Sam raced after her.

But the instant the friends set foot on the field, the storm zigzagged toward them.

"Ow!" Antonio cried. "Dirt is pelting my face!"

"It stings!" Lucy said. "We need to cover our faces!"

Sam looked down at the sash. He paused, then quickly took it off and tore it into three pieces. "Here! Use these like bandannas!" Sam yelled, as he tied a piece of the sash over his nose and mouth.

The storm was so thick that they couldn't see. But the swirling dust calmed for a moment — and they saw Ollie was gone!

"Where did Ollie go?" Antonio shouted.

Sam looked all around. "He must've been scooped up by Orson's dust storm! We need to find him!"

"It's not going to be easy!" Lucy said, as she pointed at the outfield.

Thick clouds of dirt and dust were rolling in and settling over the field. Sam could no longer see the school.

Then something small and dark appeared.

It had exited the swirling clouds and was coming toward Sam and his friends.

The kickball.

Ever so slowly, it rolled toward them.

Sam held his breath. The kickball should not have been terrifying — but it was. It was terrifying because as it rolled, it changed. It was growing and changing into something horrible . . . The ball's rubber surface spread and became thin. Hollow black eyes flashed as it spun, and a dark mouth appeared.

# DUGOUT DINNER

$T$he gigantic, monstrous kickball slowly rolled to a stop. It towered over Sam and his friends. They took a step back.

"The — the ball!" Antonio stammered. "It's — it's — it's a giant head with a face!"

A chill ran down Sam's spine. "It's the face of Orson Eerie!"

⌒74⌒

"Help!" a voice called from the dust cloud.

It was Ollie! He was caught in the spinning winds.

"We have to save him!" Lucy shouted.

"How?" Antonio asked.

Sam knew the answer. "We need to defeat Orson Eerie!"

**KRUNCH! KRUNCH!**

The monstrous ball began rolling forward again.

"Run!" Sam cried.

The ground shook as the enormous ball picked up speed and chased after them.

"We might be safe in the dugout!" Lucy shouted, and ran that way. Sam and Antonio raced after her.

Sam nearly tripped on something. Looking back, he saw the air pump he had left behind the previous morning. The ball rolled over the pump and it was gone.

*The pump!* Sam thought. *The ball ate it!*

Sam could feel the ball nipping at his heels. Any second, Orson Eerie would swallow him and his friends.

Lucy slid into the dugout. Sam and Antonio jumped in after her.

**KRASH!**

The ball slammed into the dugout's roof. The space between the roof and the dugout wall was too narrow for the ball to pass through.

The monstrous kickball was just inches from their faces. They felt Orson Eerie's hot breath. The monster was huge and horrible. It chomped and gnawed at the wooden roof.

Sam peered into the darkness of its mouth. He saw the air pump — it was broken in two.

"Orson ate the air pump — and chomped it in two!" Sam cried. "It looks like we're next!"

*T*he Orson Eerie kickball chomped and chewed the dugout roof. Then —

## CLONK! CLONK! CLONK!

There was a tremendous clattering at Sam's feet. The swirling winds had knocked over a bag of wooden baseball bats. One splintered bat tore a hole in the bag.

Lucy exclaimed, "That's it! I have a *home run of a plan.* Grab those bats! We're going to deflate that monster ball!"

"YES!" Antonio cheered. "I love a good Orson-beating plan!"

The friends scooped up as many bats as they could carry. They raced out onto the field.

**REE-ARRGGHHH!**

The monstrous ball roared. It spun and chased after Sam, Lucy, and Antonio.

"What's the plan?" Sam cried.

"This!" Lucy shouted, as she tossed a bat over her shoulder. It hit the grass.

Sam glanced behind him. The Orson Eerie ball chomped at the ground as it sped after them! The bat flew up into its mouth along with dirt and grass. The ball's fangs chewed. Wood bits flew.

"I get it!" Sam said. "Orson will swallow the bats and chomp them into sharp splinters!"

"They'll shred him up from the inside out!" Antonio said.

Sam, Lucy, and Antonio raced across the infield. Every few steps, they tossed another bat behind them. Sam heard the bats being gobbled up. The first part of the plan was working.

But then —

"Oh no!" Antonio exclaimed. "There's nowhere else to run!"

Dirt kicked up as Sam slid to a stop. The huge metal backstop was directly ahead of them — and the terrifying kickball was hurtling toward them! They were trapped.

Sam looked at his friends. They each still held two bats.

"We need Orson to swallow more bats!" Sam yelled. "Throw your bats NOW!"

They did. The scattered bats blocked the kickball's path to Sam, Lucy, and Antonio.

The monstrous ball rolled to a stop. Bits of wood fell from its teeth.

Sam gulped.

"Why did Orson stop? We need him to eat those bats," Antonio whispered. "There aren't enough giant splinters yet!"

"We need to *make* Orson come toward us," Lucy said.

Sam narrowed his eyes. "Don't worry," he growled. "I'll get him to come closer."

Sam rattled the metal backstop and shouted, "HEY, ORSON EERIE! DO YOU SEE THESE HALL MONITOR SASHES ON OUR FACES?! WE ARE *STILL* THE HALL MONITORS! WE WILL *NEVER* STOP FIGHTING YOU!"

**REE-ARRGGHHH!**

The monstrous kickball turned red with anger. It rolled forward like an unstoppable boulder. The bats disappeared! The ground quaked and the backstop shook. The ball kept rolling forward! It was going to swallow the hall monitors next! But then —

**VWIIIIIIIISH!**

A loud hissing sound. And another! And another!

"It's working!" Sam exclaimed.

Splinters of wood broke through the ball's surface! Air rushed from a dozen holes in the creepy kickball!

"The broken bats are shredding the ball!" Antonio said.

The monster's strange eyes were wide.

**AIIIEIEEE!!!**

The ball howled and whirled and spun. Orson Eerie was deflating and shrinking.

The dust storm began swirling more and more slowly. Soon, the dirt fell to the ground. The dark dust cloud was gone. But now the kindergartner was falling!

"Heeeelllp!" Ollie cried out.

# BUBBLE GUM CLEAN-UP CREW

## 15

Antonio raced across the field. "I've got him!" he shouted as he caught Ollie in his outstretched arms.

"Nice catch, Antonio!" Lucy said.

"Just like chasing pop-ups in the outfield!" he replied, setting Ollie on his feet.

Sam eyed the kickball. It was back to normal size — but it was torn and deflated. Bits of chewed-up bats lay on the ground beside it.

"Are you okay?" Antonio asked Ollie.

"Yes," the kindergartner said, nodding. "What happened? Where did all that dust come from? I couldn't see anything."

Sam and his friends weren't sure how to respond. But they didn't have to.

"There they are!" Ms. Grinker shouted as she ran toward the field. Mr. Nekobi and Principal Winik sped after her. Other teachers and students gathered on the steps to watch.

Sam tore off his piece of the hall monitor sash and shoved it into his pocket. Antonio and Lucy did the same.

"We did a head count," Principal Winik said. He panted and wiped beads of sweat from his forehead. "We realized you four were missing."

"We're safe," Sam said. He turned to Ms. Grinker. "I'm sorry we left our classroom."

"But we heard Ollie calling for help," Lucy added.

"And we could never *really* abandon our hall monitor duties, so we had to help!" Antonio said.

Sam winked at his friends.

Mr. Nekobi stepped foward. "I believe our hall monitors have saved the day."

"I agree," Principal Winik said. "In fact, I think they deserve to have their jobs back. What do you think, Ms. Grinker?"

Ms. Grinker looked at Sam, Lucy, and Antonio — one after the other. At last, she grumbled, "Yes, I guess they were brave."

"Great!" Principal Winik replied. "They are fully reinstated as hall monitors!"

"But you still need to clean up the bubble gum in my room," said Ms. Grinker.

Then she and the principal led Ollie into the school.

Sam, Lucy, and Antonio looked up at Mr. Nekobi.

"Um . . . one question," Antonio said. "How do we scrub, like, four tons of *bubble gum* from a classroom?"

Mr. Nekobi grinned. "We'll figure it out together."

Sam smiled as he and his friends marched back inside Eerie Elementary. The school was terrible and terrifying — but they were hall monitors again. And Sam knew that soon they would be called on to battle Eerie Elementary once more.

## Shhhh!

This news is top secret: **Jack Chabert** is a pen name for *New York Times*–bestselling author Max Brallier. (Max uses a made-up name instead of his real name so Orson Eerie won't come after him, too!)

Max was once a hall monitor at Joshua Eaton Elementary School in Reading, MA. But today, Max lives in a super-weird old apartment building in New York City. His days are spent writing, playing video games, and reading comic books. And at night, he walks the halls, always prepared for the moment when his building will come alive.

Max is the author of more than twenty books for children, including the middle-grade series The Last Kids on Earth and Galactic Hot Dogs. Visit the author at www.MaxBrallier.com.

**Matt Loveridge** loves illustrating children's books. When he's not painting or drawing, he likes hiking, biking, and drinking milk from the carton. He lives in the mountains of Utah with his wife and kids, and their black dog named Blue.

# HOW MUCH DO YOU KNOW ABOUT

# Eerie Elementary

## The Hall Monitors Are FIRED?

**W**hy does Orson Eerie want to get Sam and his friends fired from their hall monitor jobs? What is his big plan?

**S**am has to turn over his hall monitor sash to Principal Winik. How does he feel without it? Does the sash have powers? (Hint! Reread pages 38-39.)

**W**hat are **two** ways the school comes alive *before* the kickball game?

**H**ow do the hall monitors use wooden baseball bats to defeat Orson Eerie?

**W**rite an action-packed story where your school comes alive during a sports game. Draw pictures and use sound-effect words to help tell your story!